INTO THE UNDERWORLD

USBORNE

QUEST
of the
GODS

CLASH OF THE
DARK SERPENT

DAN HUNTER

USBORNE

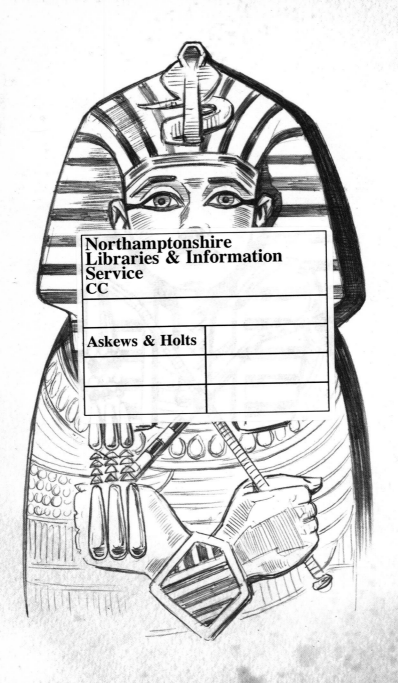

The Sacred Coffin Text of Pharaoh Akori

I shall sail rightly in my vessel
I am Lord of Eternity
in the crossing of the sky.

Let my heart speak truth;
Let me not suffer
the torments of the wicked!

For the Great Devourer awaits,
And the forty-two demons
howl around the Hall of Judgement.

Let me hold my head upright in honour,
and be spared the claws and teeth
of the Shrieking Ones.

The Eaters of Bones,
let them not touch me.
The Drinkers of Blood,
let them not come near me.
The Winged Ones with Jaws of Iron,
may they pass me by.

and may I remain safe
in the presence of Osiris forever.

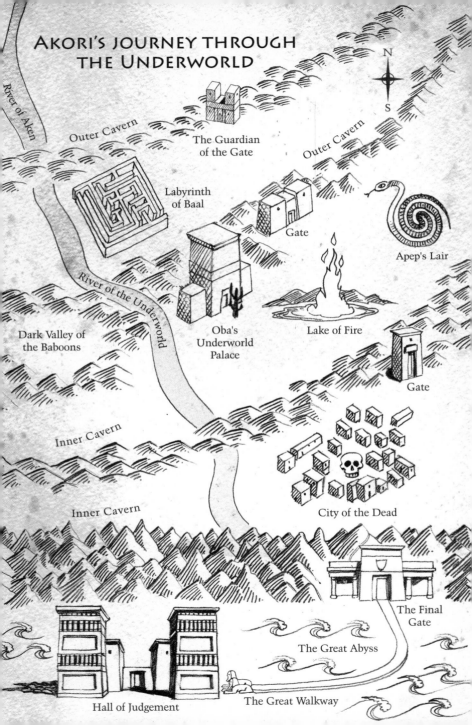

PROLOGUE

A flame blazed in a wide copper dish,
forming strange, magical images. The
demon-boy, Oba, once ruler of Egypt, now
King of the Underworld, leaned forwards and
studied the flickering fire-pictures. He saw
his enemy, Akori, leaning over a table,
playing the ancient game of seega. Oba
recognized the board immediately. Clutching
the arms of his throne with his greasy
fingers, his mouth curled into an ugly sneer.

"My game," he snarled to himself. "That
puffed-up farm boy dares to sit in my palace,
playing my game."

In the dancing flames, the image of Akori,
the young Pharaoh of Egypt, moved a stone
counter, taking his opponent's remaining

pieces with a grin of triumph. Opposite him, a skinny, bald boy – Akori's High Priest, Manu – shrugged and crossed his arms in defeat.

Oba's sneer turned into a hoarse croak of rage. "That High Priest must be some kind of drooling idiot to be beaten by a filthy peasant. Either that, or he's letting him win."

Oba got up and began to pace the floor, his blood boiling with anger and frustration. "I'll make that farm boy pay for his insolence," he spat. "He sits on the throne of Egypt – my throne – a common peasant, pretending he is the real Pharaoh while his grovelling priest allows him to win. It would be different if I was there. If he was playing against me…"

Oba fell silent as he imagined capturing Akori and seizing the throne of Egypt once *more. He looked around the dark chamber with grim satisfaction. Columns of black stone, carved with ancient hieroglyphs of death and destruction, rose into the gloom. The fire gave the only light, sending curls of foul-smelling smoke around the room and causing sinister shadows to crawl across the walls.*

"When my army of the dead conquers Egypt I will take my palace back," Oba hissed. "I will take back everything that belongs to me. I'll teach that farm boy his proper place – chained up in my dungeon!"

A loud crash interrupted Oba, shaking the floor beneath his feet. Scowling, he whirled around to see a tall, heavily muscled figure outlined against the fire. Oba's ally, Set, Lord of Storms, stepped forward and bared his razor-sharp teeth.

Oba shivered, fear leaving a trail of

goosebumps across his skin. Annoyed at himself for being afraid, he snapped, "What is it?"

The God crossed his arms across his chest and tilted his grotesque head to one side. His eyes were jet-black pools of evil.

For a moment there was silence. Oba realized he had gone too far and his heart began to pound. Finally, Set spoke, his deep voice echoing eerily around the room. "You live because I wish you to live. Do not make me wish otherwise. Three times you have failed me, and my patience wears thin."

Oba gritted his teeth. "I am sorry, My Lord Set. I did not mean to offend you."

There was no reply, Set just glared at him as if he were an insect.

"It is time," the God said, eventually. "Akori will soon return to the Underworld. Is the trap ready?"

Oba nodded. "Yes," he said, eagerly. "This time I'll deal with Akori once and for all. This time, he will die." A hungry smile spread across his face. "And I cannot think of anything that will bring me more pleasure."

"A pleasure we will share," said Set with a low, menacing growl.

CHAPTER ONE

Sunlight streamed into a walled courtyard within the Pharaoh's palace, sparkling on a pool of clear, cool water. Close by, beneath the leafy shade of a persea tree, the chief servant placed three goblets of grape juice and a dish of water on a stone table.

"Thank you," Akori said, looking up from the *seega* board and giving the servant a grateful smile.

"Your Majesty is welcome," the servant

replied with a bow. "If there is anything else you need…"

"I'm fine, unless you can give me some help winning this game."

A smile flickered across the chief servant's face. "I am sure Your Majesty needs no help to defeat his opponents," he said.

"If only that were true," groaned Akori, gazing at the board.

"Ha, you might have beaten me before, but this game is *mine*," grinned Manu, opposite. He moved a red counter forwards with a click. "Surrounded in three places," he smirked, removing three of Akori's blue counters.

The former High Priest of Horus, who sat next to Manu, smiled.

"The game's not over yet," Akori replied. Leaning forwards, he studied the board closely. He had twelve of his blue counters left. Manu had sixteen and his position was much stronger – one of his counters was in place to take yet another piece. Akori moved it to safety.

Quick as a flash, Manu moved a different stone. "Another two blues to me," he said. "Looks like I'm going to break your winning streak at last."

"My old pupil learns fast," said the old High Priest of Horus. He looked thin and frail, but his lined face was lit by an inner strength. Ever since the evil God Set and demon-boy Oba had begun their campaign of revenge, he had been one of Akori's most trusted advisors. Akori didn't know what he would do without the old man's wisdom and experience.

With a purr, an elegant pale cat jumped onto the table. For a moment she lapped at the dish of water while peering at the board.

Then she looked up at Akori, and mewed pitifully, before jumping to the floor and sitting at his feet expectantly.

"Great, Ebe thinks I'm going to lose too," sighed Akori.

"Your mind is clouded," said the old priest. "You move your pieces too quickly and pay no attention to Manu's strategy."

Akori glanced up, amazed as always that the old man sensed so much despite his blind eyes. "It's hard to concentrate, knowing that in a few hours, when the sun sets, we'll be going back to the Underworld," he replied. "Who knows what traps Oba has set for us this time?" He ran his fingers across the three gems that glittered on the collar of his golden armour. Each of the Pharaoh Stones held a certain power – courage, speed and strength. He had won them from Gods who had taken Oba's side. But only when he had collected all five of the gems could he hope to defeat Oba and Set, and release Osiris, the real ruler of the Underworld, from the terrible prison Set had made for him. Until then, Oba reigned in the Underworld and was building an army of the dead to send against Egypt.

Akori had challenged Manu to play *seega* in the hope of forgetting about his impending quest for an hour or two. Instead, his thoughts kept returning to the dangers of the Underworld and the Gods he had battled there. Akori's jittery mood wasn't caused by fear, but by frustration. All the time he was sitting around playing games, Oba was growing in power. With every passing hour he became a bigger threat to Egypt.

I should be doing something, Akori thought to himself. *Anything but sitting here.*

"Where's Horus? Why hasn't he...?" Akori

fell silent as the old High Priest held up his thin, bony hand.

"I understand that your soul burns to defeat Oba and Set and make Egypt safe," the old man said. "But the quest before you is like this game of *seega*. You must keep your mind cool. See your enemy's moves before he makes them. In your impatience you make foolish mistakes. When this happens on the *seega* board you will only lose a game, but if you do not think clearly in the Underworld…well, then you will lose your life." Despite the seriousness of his words, a smile suddenly lit up the old man's face. "You cannot travel to the Underworld before sunset. Until then, a wise man would enjoy the sunshine and the company of friends."

Akori frowned. "Sorry," he murmured. "But it is difficult to relax when your kingdom is under threat from an insane murderer who is about to unleash an army of the dead."

"Clear your mind," the old priest repeated with a wry smile. "Worry serves no useful purpose. It only brings confusion."

Closing his eyes with a sigh, Akori lifted his face to the blazing Egyptian sun, which filtered through the leafy shade of the tree. He felt its warmth burning away his frustration. The old priest was right. There was nothing he could do about Oba right now and there were still a few hours left before he had to travel to the Underworld. Why not enjoy the afternoon?

"Clear your mind all you like," he heard Manu say. "I'm still going to win this…" His voice trailed off into a gasp.

Suddenly, the warmth on Akori's face disappeared. He opened his eyes and looked around. He could scarcely believe it. He closed his eyes and opened them again. But it was true. Everything *had* changed.

The world had been plunged into darkness. The sun had vanished and the sky was as black as coal. Not even a single star lit the unnatural night.

This can't be right, Akori thought, jumping to his feet. *I must have fallen asleep. I have to be dreaming...*

For almost a minute the world seemed to hold its breath. Then, from somewhere in the palace, came a scream. Another joined it. Then another.

"The sun has gone out. It is the end of the world!" a woman's voice shrieked.

"Dead, we're all *dead*. Anubis is coming for us," a man yelled.

"Horus have mercy," another man wept.

Keep a cool head, Akori told himself firmly, even though his heart was pounding.

You are the Pharaoh. Whatever has happened it is up to you to solve it. He looked down at Manu and the old priest. "Somehow, Ra's sun-barge has been pulled out of the sky," he said, trying to sound calm. "And I know of only one person who would do such a thing."

Ebe jumped onto his shoulder, hissing.

Manu looked up at Akori, his face pale in the darkness. "Oba," he said, his voice wavering.

CHAPTER TWO

"Your Majesty," the chief servant cried, rushing into the courtyard. "What has happened? Where is the sun? Is the world truly ending?"

Even in the darkness, Akori could see that he was trembling violently. He placed his hand on the servant's shoulder. "The world is not ending, not if I have anything to do with it. But dark forces are at work. I need you to keep the staff calm while I find out how to stop them. Do you think you can do that?"

The chief servant recovered himself. "Of course, Your Majesty," he said, bowing his head. "You can count on me."

"I know," replied Akori, squeezing the man's shoulder. "Tell them that every lamp and torch must be lit. I want the people in the city outside to see the palace blazing with light. Tell them their Pharaoh will return the sun to Egypt. All will be well soon."

"What are we going to do?" Manu asked nervously as the servant rushed off to carry out his orders.

"We'll go to the palace shrine," Akori told him. "Horus will guide us."

"Now you are thinking clearly," said the old priest, rising to his feet.

Akori led the way through the palace's passages towards the shrine, trying to control his own fear. If Oba was able to snatch the sun from the sky, his power was even greater than Akori had thought. He shivered. The dark seemed to be closing in on him, bringing with it the cold of a desert night. Could it also bring an attack by Oba and the undead?

Before long, the chief servant's orders spread around the palace and the screams died down. Ahead of Akori, dark passages began to glow with light as servants scurried from lamp to lamp. Then finally, he saw the great doors of the palace shrine.

As Akori pushed the doors open, darkness seemed to roll out in a wave. Taking a blazing torch from the wall, he entered the great hall, striding past carved columns towards the massive statue of falcon-headed Horus. The old priest, Ebe and Manu followed.

"Lord Horus," he heard Manu whisper behind him. "Hear our prayers. Evil magic threatens all Egypt. Help your champion bring back the sun."

"Guide us through the darkness and give me the strength to stop Oba," Akori added. He held up the torch. Shadows flickered across the face of the statue, making it look as if it was moving.

Akori's eyes widened. The statue *was* moving. The stone was coming alive!

There was a thunderous roar like an earthquake ripping through stone as the great falcon-headed God stepped from the statue. "Light!" Horus commanded. His voice shook the great columns.

At once the air shimmered with golden rays. Akori gazed up at the God. Horus was so gigantic that his head was almost touching the ceiling high above. Akori barely came up to the great God's knee. Lowering his torch, he bowed. "Lord Horus, help me.

27

The sun is gone. If we cannot bring it back the crops will fail. People will starve. Already, they are terrified."

Horus looked down at him, his eyes glowing gold. "Some of the great Gods have been tricked into joining Oba and Set," he boomed. "You have beaten three of them, and won three of the Pharaoh Stones. To win the fourth you must battle an enemy greater than any you have yet faced, for only Apep has the power to capture the Sun God."

Akori felt the blood drain from his face. Even though he wasn't a great scholar like Manu, he had heard of Apep. Everyone had. At the end of every day, as Ra's barge sank towards the Underworld where it would spend the night, Apep, the great Snake God, attacked. The priests said that if Apep ever defeated Ra, darkness would fall across the world for ever.

"But how did he do it?" Manu asked, stepping forward to stand beside Akori. "Apep can only attack when Ra's barge enters the Underworld. The sun disappeared in the middle of the afternoon, when it was still high in the sky."

Horus turned his great head to look at Manu. "Every day that my father, Osiris, the rightful ruler of the Underworld, remains in Set's prison, Oba's power grows stronger," he explained. "He must have broken the spells that kept Apep in the Underworld and released him to attack Ra."

Akori saw pain in Horus's face when he mentioned his father. He imagined how he would feel if Oba and Set had captured someone he loved – Manu or Ebe or the old High Priest – and he became more determined than ever to stop Oba.

"Lord Horus," he said, firmly. "I will

release your father. I will fight Oba and Set with every last breath in my body."

Horus looked down on him. "I thank you, my champion. But first you must release Ra and win the fourth Pharaoh Stone. Without all five Stones your quest is lost."

Akori's hand reached down, touching the hilt of the curved *khopesh* sword that hung at his side. Coloured light glittered from the Pharaoh Stones in the collar of his magical armour. "Then I will return to the Underworld as soon as possible," he said quietly.

Manu nodded thoughtfully. "Since the sun will not set today, could we go now?" he asked. "You're ready, aren't you, Ebe?"

Ebe twined herself around Akori's legs, purring.

Akori couldn't help smiling. What had he done to deserve friends like this? Knowing they were by his side gave Akori courage that even a Pharaoh Stone couldn't match.

"I can help you on your way," boomed Horus, interrupting Akori's thoughts. "But I must warn you, Apep is a terrible foe. When you stand before him, you will need more than courage or speed or strength to save you."

CHAPTER THREE

Akori gripped the hilt of his *khopesh* tightly as Horus's words sank in. Even the Pharaoh Stones he had won would not be enough to defeat the mighty Snake God Apep. He bowed his head. "Whatever it takes, I vow to you, Lord Horus, I will not fail."

"Destiny has given me a fine champion." Horus's voice was full of pride. He bent down, opening one massive hand. "Take this scroll from Thoth, God of Wisdom. It will aid you."

Akori took a yellowed scroll from Horus's palm. "How do we get to the Underworld now that the sun has gone?" he asked.

Horus's falcon head tilted to one side. "The barriers between the worlds of the dead and the living are weakening," he said. "Oba and Set will tear them down completely when they send their army against you. Already it becomes easier to slip through the seams. But you can use this to your advantage. Enter the Underworld using the secret doorway created by the Dark Pharaoh, as you did on your last quest. But you will not need a spell to open the door this time. The borders of the Underworld are so fragile that the words on this scroll should transport you straight there."

"That sounds easy enough," Akori replied, secretly relieved that he wouldn't have to use his own tomb, as he had before. Climbing inside his coffin gave him the creeps.

Shaking his head, Horus replied, "It will not be easy, Akori. The dead are unable to find peace with Osiris imprisoned. They are angry and restless."

Akori gulped, remembering his fight with the dead Pharaoh Amenhotep. Oba had sent the mummy as an assassin to kill him. The memory of Amenhotep's tattered flesh and the beetles crawling from his eye sockets sent a shudder down Akori's spine. The dead were fierce, and difficult to destroy. Putting the thought to the back of his mind, he said, "Is there anything else we need to know, Lord Horus?"

"Only that you take my blessings with you as always." The mighty God raised his hand. "I bid you, and your companions, farewell. All of you have my gratitude."

Ebe purred at Akori's feet. Akori noticed

that Manu was blushing. For the High Priest of Horus to win the gratitude of the God he served was an overwhelming honour. "Thank you, My Lord," Manu muttered.

Horus stepped back inside his statue. The light faded, plunging the shrine back into darkness. The God was gone.

Akori lifted his torch, turning to face the old priest. "We must leave now," he said, quickly. "Can I ask you to look after things while I'm gone?"

The priest nodded. "It will be an honour to do so."

Akori smiled at him gratefully. "Thank you. It will be difficult to stop people panicking."

"I will tell them the truth," the priest replied. "That their Pharaoh has gone to set the sun back in the sky. It will give them hope."

Akori nodded. "We will be back as quickly as we can," he said.

After the old priest had blessed them and headed back into the palace, Manu unrolled the scroll, and read the travelling spell to take them to the palace of the Dark Pharaoh. Although they had used the spell to get there in their last quest, the sensation of travelling without moving still felt strange to Akori. With a bump, the three friends arrived in the gloomy ruined palace. Here, in the eerie darkness, centuries of deathly silence filled the passages and chambers. Even though he had been here once before, Akori still couldn't help shivering.

Behind him, Manu cleared his throat. "Umm…before we go any further, I should probably tell you some things about Apep," he said, nervously.

"Like what?" Akori asked, brushing a huge dusty cobweb aside.

"Well, for a start, although we know he

takes the form of a giant snake, no two scrolls agree on his exact size," Manu replied. "Only one thing's for sure. They all say he's big."

"How big?"

Manu cleared his throat again, sounding uncomfortable. "One scroll says forty royal cubits."

In his mind, Akori pictured a snake longer than ten tall men. "That *is* big," he muttered, heart sinking.

"All the other scrolls say much, *much* bigger," Manu continued. "Big enough to circle the world and to swallow the sun whole."

Akori stared at Manu in disbelief, one eyebrow raised. "Is there anything else you can tell me?" he asked.

"Well, he's Set's oldest ally and he's...um... sort of...impossible to kill. Only a God of equal power would be able to destroy him.

And as he's one of the most powerful Gods in existence..." Manu looked at Akori apologetically.

"I meant, is there anything you can tell me that might help me fight him?" said Akori with a sigh.

Manu shook his head. "Not really. Sorry."

Akori touched the three Stones in his collar, reminding himself that he had already defeated Oba and his corrupted Gods three times. Feeling slightly braver, he gave Manu a small smile. But inside, Akori could feel his nerves building. He wondered what new horrors awaited them in the Underworld. Oba's army of the dead would be even bigger by now, and even stronger. They paused by the Dark Pharaoh's doorway.

"You read the spell, you're better with words," Akori said to Manu.

With shaking fingers, Manu unrolled the

ancient paper and raised his voice:

"*Gods of the night, hear my command:*
Lift the veil. Let mortals through.
Into the darkness, where Osiris rules..."

The spell went on and on, Manu's voice sometimes pleading, sometimes commanding. Akori tensed, fingers clutching the hilt of his *khopesh*, waiting to be whisked to the Underworld, ready to fight.

Finally, Manu finished. He let the scroll drop to his side, looking around in confusion.

"Nothing's happening," Akori whispered. "Are you sure you read it properly?"

Manu checked the scroll, opening his mouth to speak. But all that came out was a shout of shock as the slab of rock beneath their feet suddenly tilted. Instantly, the three friends began plummeting downwards.

"Manu! Ebe!" Akori yelled as he was

pulled down, arms thrashing, faster and faster.

He tried shouting again but it felt as if all the air had been sucked from his lungs. He fell deeper and deeper, like he was dropping down into an endless well. It was so dark Akori couldn't see the others. He couldn't hear them either. He was falling so fast now all he could hear was the roar of the air rushing past his ears.

Then, as suddenly as it had begun, the falling stopped, and Akori hit the ground with a jolt.

"Hey, careful. You nearly flattened me!"

Akori opened his eyes, and saw Manu sprawled on the floor beneath him, with Ebe in his arms.

"S-sorry," stuttered Akori. "Are you both okay?"

"Horus wasn't joking about this not being

easy," Manu replied, managing a feeble smile. "I think I almost preferred travelling in your coffin."

"Where are we?" Akori glanced around. They were inside a dark and dingy chamber, lit by one meagre torch. But there was something oddly familiar about the room. It reminded Akori of a room in his own palace, decorated with pictures depicting the stories of the lives of the Pharaohs. Akori peered through the gloom at his surroundings. Paintings covered these walls too, but instead they showed gruesome images of his ancestors in torment and agony. In one corner, Akori noticed a vast ornamental chest, similar to one in his own palace. The lid was open, but where Akori's featured a picture of him riding in a chariot, this chest showed the young Pharaoh, chained in a prison.

43

Akori gasped. "We're back," he whispered. "This is Oba's palace." He shuddered despite himself. "Let's get out of here," he said. "I don't like the feel of this place."

Staying close together, Akori, Manu and Ebe slowly crept through the palace corridors. The darkness seemed to clutch at Akori, whispering evil into his ear. Red-eyed spiders squatted in cobwebs, spitting as the three travellers passed by. Akori glanced at one of the pictures on the wall. It showed the fate that awaited the unworthy in the Underworld – the gaping jaws of Ammit the Devourer, eater of souls. He shuddered.

At last, they reached the shrine. Akori looked around. It was identical to his own shrine in shape and size, but where the statue of Horus should have been was a heap of broken rubble and the walls and columns were scrawled with hideous curses.

The gloomy air hung with a stench that clung to Akori's nostrils and made him feel sick.

From the look on Manu's face, Akori knew his friend was even more horrified than he was. Quietly, he touched his shoulder. "It could be worse," he said. "At least we haven't had to fight the dead."

They all froze as they heard a terrible rasping sound, growing louder and closer by the second. Spinning around, Akori saw a figure staggering towards them. It was wearing priest's robes which hung in rags, showing the pale, worm-eaten flesh beneath. The hilt of a dagger jutted from its chest. A raw scar zigzagged across its face.

At Akori's feet, Ebe hissed and snarled. In reply, the monstrous figure opened its mouth, making a grotesque, gargling sound.

"Oh no!" Manu turned to Akori his eyes

wide with fear. "It's Oba's evil priest, Bukhu, risen from the dead," he gasped. "He tried to kill me!"

CHAPTER FOUR

Akori watched as their undead attacker
lurched towards them, the dagger buried
deep in his chest. Akori gave a shudder of
recognition. Manu was right. In Egypt, when
Oba was still Pharaoh, Bukhu, the High
Priest of Set, had been his closest ally. The
last time Akori had seen him, Bukhu had
tried to block his path to Oba, using Manu
as a human shield. He had threatened to
cut Manu's throat, but the young priest had
escaped his clutches. In fury, Bukhu had

thrown his dagger at Akori but it had rebounded from his shield and buried itself in Bukhu's heart instead, where it still remained.

Bukhu glared at Akori and opened his mouth wide, revealing the blackened stumps of his teeth. A screech of pure hate echoed around the temple as Bukhu's fingers plucked the weapon from his heart. Maggots spilled from the open wound. "Revenge!" Bukhu muttered. His voice rose to a cry of mad hatred as he staggered through the gloom, dagger held high.

Akori passed the burning torch he was holding to Manu. He drew his golden *khopesh*. Stepping forward to protect Manu and Ebe, he sank into a warrior's crouch. "I would have let you live, Bukhu," he said grimly. "It was your own foolishness that killed you."

The words seemed to anger Bukhu even more. Howling, he launched himself at Akori, the dagger blurring in the air as it slashed at his throat.

Akori dodged to one side, his *khopesh* blocking the blow. Bukhu staggered. Recovering quickly, he turned back to Akori with an even angrier snarl of *"Revenge!"* and threw himself into a fresh attack.

The *khopesh* sang through the air once more. Sparks flew as metal met metal. In death, Bukhu's vicious rage had given him more strength than he ever possessed when he was alive. This time, Akori was forced back. Knocked off balance, he tripped over a piece of rock. Sprawling awkwardly on his back, he dropped the *khopesh*. It skittered away across the floor.

Both Bukhu's ragged hands now clutched the hilt of the dagger. *"Die!"* he screeched, staggering forward to plunge it into Akori's heart.

"You'll have to kill me first," yelled Manu, jumping over Akori to battle Bukhu.

Bukhu turned at the sound of a deep, rumbling roar. Ebe had transformed. As the Goddess Bast, she had become a gigantic wildcat. Bukhu was now trapped between the two of them.

The dagger gleamed as its edge caught the light. Bukhu turned this way and that, trying to find his escape. "You," he rasped at Manu. "I should have spilled your life's blood when I had the chance – cut your throat and let it pour out onto the sand."

His gaze flickered to Ebe. "And Bast. Even a Goddess is not safe in my temple of hate. You will both die. By my hand."

"Not while I am alive," said Akori, scrambling to his feet.

"Then I'll kill you first," Bukhu said to Akori, before grabbing a handful of dust and gravel, and flinging it in Manu's face.

With a shout of shock and pain, Manu dropped the torch and sank to his knees, wiping grit from his streaming eyes.

Snarling, Ebe pounced into darkness, but the dead priest was no longer there. Bukhu had hurled himself at Akori, tattered rags streaming out behind him.

Akori ducked to one side. The dagger's blade glanced off the golden collar at his throat as the full weight of Bukhu slammed into him. Instinctively, he grabbed his opponent's wrist.

As Bukhu's weight bore him to the ground, Akori reached out, clutching a handful of rags and bringing his opponent down with him. Over and over, they rolled, wrestling for the knife. Akori's head hit a broken rock, dazing him for a second. His stomach turned as a foul smell hit him. It was Bukhu's breath. The dead man's face was so close to his own, his rotten teeth snapping at the air. Bukhu was trying to bite him! Just in time, Akori's fingers curled around his throat, holding him off.

Bukhu pulled the dagger back to strike again.

The Pharaoh Stones, Akori told himself desperately as he struggled. If only he could touch one of them the extra surge of magical speed or strength would be enough to overcome the priest. But he needed both hands to fight Bukhu. There had to be another way. As he tumbled across the floor, holding off the shrieking Bukhu, Akori forced himself to think.

The answer came as Bukhu rolled on top of him. Grunting with effort, he began

53

edging the dagger, bit by bit, towards Akori's unprotected face.

His muscles burning, Akori strained. Closer and closer, the dagger came, until its deadly tip was almost touching Akori's eye.

"*Revenge,*" hissed Bukhu.

"No!" With every last ounce of his strength, Akori heaved himself to one side, jerking his head away.

The dagger smashed into the ground in a spray of sparks. Cursing, Bukhu raised it again.

He was too slow. Releasing his grip on Bukhu's wrist, Akori shoved him as hard as he could. Howling with pain, Bukhu fell back, allowing Akori to twist out from beneath him.

Scrambling to his feet, Akori leaped up the heap of rubble.

Bukhu rose. "Coward," he spat, his voice

like the cracking of bones. "You will not escape me."

In the shadows, Akori heard Ebe growl with soft menace. "No, Ebe, leave him," he said softly.

"Yes, little Goddess, your turn will come," snarled Bukhu in reply. "Let us end this."

"Ha!" Akori shouted at Bukhu. "You couldn't end this the first time and you're not going to end it this time either."

Bukhu's growls reached a deafening roar.

"Why did you say that?" Manu hissed. "Now you've made him even madder."

"It's all right," Akori whispered. "I've got a plan."

"Come on!" he yelled at Bukhu. "What are you waiting for?"

As Bukhu started charging towards him, Akori lifted his fingers in the darkness to touch the Stone of Speed on his collar.

Energy surged through him and he flitted backwards, away from Bukhu's lunging arms. "Too slow," he taunted.

Bukhu shook his arms in fury, causing clouds of dust to fill the air.

Akori raced back through the palace to the first room they had arrived in, with Bukhu in furious pursuit.

"Why are you going back down there?" Manu cried. But Akori ignored him. He had to – he couldn't let Bukhu know what he had planned.

Down in the passageway Bukhu's roars echoed even louder through the darkness. Akori sped back past the picture of the monstrous Ammit. He was moving so fast the cobwebs were blown from the walls.

"Is that as fast as you can go?" he yelled over his shoulder at Bukhu as he reached the room.

"Insolent wretch!" Bukhu screeched. "Wait and see how slowly I kill you. It will be agony."

Akori crouched in the darkness beside the door. As Bukhu came charging into the room, Akori extended his leg. There was a yell, followed by a thud as Bukhu tripped and went flying into the open chest. Quick as a flash, Akori touched the Stone of Strength before racing over and slamming the stone lid shut.

"Nooooooo!" Bukhu cried, his hands pummelling the lid. But it was too heavy. Bukhu's yells became fainter and fainter. And then, finally, the monstrous priest fell silent.

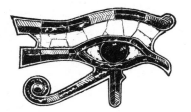

CHAPTER FIVE

Akori felt a hand on his shoulder. He turned and saw Manu right behind him, his eyes wide with awe. Ebe, who had returned to her small form, wound herself around Akori's legs and purred with pride.

Akori smiled at his friends gratefully. Then he adjusted his armour. "Come on," he said. "I have to get my *khopesh*. Then we'd better get moving."

Once Akori had retrieved his sword they cautiously ventured further through Oba's dark palace. Akori scanned the passage beyond, watching for more attackers. In the distance he could hear wind moaning around the walls and the groans of dead slaves.

"Apep won't be here," Manu continued. "The scrolls all say that he dwells in the caverns. We'll have to find our way out."

"The quickest way is by the courtyard," said Akori.

Manu gulped. "But that's the busiest part of the palace..." His voice trailed off.

Akori gripped the hilt of his *khopesh*. "We'll be careful," he said, quietly. "Come on, it's not far."

Keeping to the deepest shadows and treading softly, Akori led Manu and Ebe along the passage that led to the courtyard. Halfway there he heard a scratching sound. He froze, his skin prickling with fear, until a skeletal rat scuttled past. Ebe's golden eyes glowed and she mewed quietly.

"There's no time for hunting. We have to rescue Ra, remember?" Akori told her.

She walked past him, her head high and the tip of her tail twitching haughtily.

"Once we're through the courtyard, it's just a short way to the caverns," Akori said.

Holding his breath, and back pressed into the wall, Akori peered around the arched gate that led into the courtyard. His eyes widened. He had been expecting something different from the splashing fountains and sweet-smelling blossoms he enjoyed at home, but the Underworld courtyard shocked him to his core.

Manu gasped beside him. "Are you sure there isn't another way through?"

Akori shook his head, eyes fixed on the scene in front of him. Before them was a thick forest of cacti. Tall, dark green columns rose towards a boiling grey sky. Each cactus had long sinewy arms, covered in spikes the size of a man's fingers. Where there would usually have been elegant columns lining the edge of the courtyard and leading out into the open, here, every escape route was blocked by the monstrous cacti.

"I really *hate* this place," Manu muttered.

"We'll just have to be careful not to touch them," Akori said. "Take it slowly. Watch every footstep." Akori edged into the lethal thicket, trying to keep his eyes on every spike ahead of him. They looked sharp enough to slide through skin like needles.

Hardly daring to breathe, Akori inched his way through the cacti, twisting his body this way and that to avoid the spikes. Every few steps he stopped and looked back. Manu's forehead was furrowed in a frown of concentration, but he was keeping up, with

Ebe slinking along at his feet. Akori's heart lifted. It was slow going but it looked like they were going to make it unharmed.

His hope was dashed by a sharp cry behind him. Whirling round, he saw Manu clutching his arm, blood seeping through his fingers. "Manu, you're hurt," he cried, starting back towards his friend.

Ebe twined herself around Manu's legs, mewing in concern.

"Stay where you are," Manu shouted.

Standing still as a statue, Akori looked into his friend's eyes – and saw pure fear.

"The cactus," Manu hissed. "It...it *moved*. It stabbed me."

Akori frowned. "That's impossible. You just didn't see the spike. It must have been an accident."

"No...I...look out!"

Akori saw a sudden movement from the

corner of his eye. He watched in horror as, with a horrible creaking sound, the cactus closest to him stretched out an arm. A spike struck his armour. Shaking his head in disbelief, he leaped backwards to protect Manu and Ebe. Even a Goddess would have no protection from these stabbing monsters.

The cacti closest to them were all moving now: limbs swinging to stab and stab again. Akori struck out with the *khopesh*, slicing through the dark green arms, but there were always more. One of them lurched forwards, an arm sweeping low. Akori blocked the blow just in time. One false move and he would be stabbed. Behind him, Manu cried out again. Akori swung the *khopesh* through the air, slashing more spikes, but there were too many. Another spike sliced the back of

65

Manu's leg. Tears in his eyes, he sank to his knees. Instantly more cacti leaned towards him, like vultures swooping for their prey.

Akori slashed at them and severed spikes fell like rain. Another cactus leaned in to attack Akori but this time he managed to swerve out of its way and it stabbed another cactus instead. There was the terrible sound of something ripping, almost as if the cactus itself was hissing with pain. Both cacti writhed together, unable to break free.

Akori felt a sudden surge of hope. "Get ready to follow me," he called over his shoulder to Manu and Ebe. Then he brandished his *khopesh* at the next cactus along. The cactus immediately lunged its gnarly arms at him, but Akori ducked and once again, the spikes embedded themselves in the flesh of the cactus next to him.

"Forward," Akori commanded and, as the

cacti struggled in vain to free themselves, the three friends edged past.

Slowly they made their way across the courtyard, with Akori using all of his skill with the *khopesh* to trick the cacti into attacking each other.

"Akori, you are a genius!" Manu exclaimed, as, one by one, the cacti became stuck together. Ebe purred her agreement. Akori gave a relieved smile as they finally emerged from the courtyard.

But his relief was soon replaced by a sense of dread. An ugly figure, slouched on a black throne a little way in front of them, began clapping slowly.

"Very good, farm boy," Oba sneered. "I'm almost impressed. But don't get too sure of yourself. You might be able to outwit some dumb plants, but you'll never outwit me."

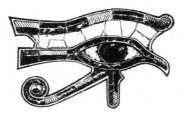

CHAPTER SIX

Akori clutched the hilt of the *khopesh* until his knuckles were white. His eyes fixed on the demon-boy, Oba.

Behind him, Manu gasped and Ebe hissed. But Akori hardly heard. He took a step forward, then another. Within a second he was running. "This time not even Set will save you," he yelled.

Oba leaned back in his throne, a contemptuous smile on his face.

Akori raced towards his enemy, his

speed increasing with every step. Horus was wrong: he didn't need the Pharaoh Stones to defeat Oba. Just one swing of the *khopesh* would do it. "And I'll wipe that smile off your face," he yelled, raising his weapon high, preparing to strike.

"Oh, I don't think so," Oba replied, coolly.

Akori heard a muffled cry behind him, then the grating of stone on stone and a desperate yowling. He looked around wildly, just in time to see Ebe clawing at the stone beneath her paws. It was sliding open, like a trapdoor. Ebe tried to scramble off but it was too smooth. Before Akori could do anything, she fell through the trapdoor into the darkness below. The door slammed shut.

Meanwhile, Manu was being held in a

vice-like grip, his face contorted with pain. His captor was like nothing Akori had seen before. Its face was haggard and ugly, with leathery skin and an evil grin that stretched from ear to ear. Yellow, slit eyes, like a snake's, stared at Akori. It had a warrior's muscular body and wore an iron breastplate and a winged helmet. Around its waist was a dirty white kilt.

Akori's shoulders sagged.

"Meet Mot, one of my demon slaves," Oba said behind him, answering Akori's unasked question. Raising his voice, he called out, "Slave, a little more pain."

Manu screamed as the demon wrenched his arm behind his back.

Akori stepped towards them, raising his *khopesh*.

"One more step and I'll order it to rip your friend's arm off," Oba hissed.

His jaw clenched in fury, Akori stopped and turned.

Oba clapped his hands together, delighted. "And, in case you were wondering, your cat is trapped in a dungeon. I can't have a Goddess wandering around loose. Even a mangy little Goddess like Bast."

Akori didn't reply. Jaw clenched, he glared at Oba.

Oba smiled back at him, clearly enjoying every moment. "There is a chance I might let them live, though," he said.

With a lazy hand Oba waved at a *seega* board that had been set up beside his throne. Opposite it was a small wooden stool.

"How about we play for your pathetic friend's life?" he continued. "If you win, he keeps his life, but if you lose, he loses his head."

"Don't do it, Akori," Manu cried. "You can't trust him."

Oba glared and flicked a hand towards the demon slave. Manu's protests were cut off by fresh screams.

Horrified, Akori looked from the *seega* board to Oba. "You're mad," he said quietly. "Completely insane."

"Your choice," Oba shrugged. "If you don't want to play, I'll have the slave kill him now. It will be fun to watch, don't you think?"

Akori heard the demon slave gurgle hungrily. "No!" he shouted. Having no other choice, he crossed quickly to the small stool and sat. "If I win, you'll let Manu go?" he asked.

Oba shrugged again. "You won't win," he answered. Resting an elbow on the arm of the throne he cupped his chin in one hand and grinned down at Akori. "I hope your stool is comfortable," he said. "It's the kind of furniture you farm people are used to, isn't it?"

An angry reply formed on Akori's lips. He bit it back, guessing that Oba was trying to make him lose his temper so that he would play badly. Once again, the old priest's words came back to him: *You must keep your mind cool. See your enemy's moves before he makes them.* A plan began to form in his mind – a way to make Oba lose *his* cool. "So, you're playing blue, I'm red?" he asked. "Does that mean you go first?"

Oba sighed. "No, farm boy, red goes first," he said. "You do know the rules, don't you?"

"I'm just learning," Akori mumbled. Reaching out, he moved a red stone forward.

It was a bad move, and he could tell Oba knew it. Moving a blue piece forward, Oba called out to Manu, "I hope you're not too attached to your head. Your friend might win against the pigs on his farm, but not against a *real* Pharaoh."

Akori felt his anger rising again, and forced it down. *Keep calm, keep calm*, he repeated to himself. He scratched his head for a moment, pretending to look confused, then moved the same stone forward again.

"Set's teeth, you're even worse than I thought you'd be," howled Oba. With a click he moved another blue stone forward. Akori's piece was surrounded on two sides. Crowing with delight, Oba removed it from the board. "You play like the ignorant peasant you really are," he sneered.

"Stop saying that. I'm the King of Egypt," Akori snapped. Reaching out he pushed another piece forward, fury flaring in his eyes.

The corner of Oba's mouth twitched. "A

real Pharaoh doesn't just wear a crown," he said smoothly. A real Pharaoh wields *power*. Like I did when I had your uncle killed."

Akori felt blood rush to his face. His fists clenched. *Keep your mind cool*, he reminded himself as Oba moved again. Quickly, he responded with a move of his own, slamming the stone down on the board, trying to make it look as if he was furious.

Once more, Oba laughed. "Another two pieces to me," he called out.

Akori could hear the demon slave licking its lips behind him. Manu groaned.

Move followed move. Each time Akori pushed a piece forward, Oba laughed in disbelief at his stupidity. Meanwhile Akori pretended to become more and more angry, moving pieces as if at random.

"You only have eight stones left," said Oba eventually. "I have all mine. This is getting boring. If you give up now I'll let your friend die quickly."

Frowning, Akori stared directly into Oba's mocking eyes. Without looking down at the board his finger moved a stone forward gently. "What happens if I do this?" he asked.

Oba glanced down at the board. A jeer died on his lips. "Impossible," he whispered.

"That's one, two...three blue stones, surrounded, isn't it?" said Akori, lifting them from the board one by one.

"A fluke," snarled Oba, moving again.

Instantly, Akori moved another stone. This time two of Oba's disappeared. Akori felt a rush of triumph. His plan had worked. It hadn't taken much to fool Oba into thinking he was just a stupid farm boy – it was what he already believed. Oba had been so sure he would win that he had forgotten all about strategy, moving his stones in wild attacks and failing to notice that Akori's angry, random moves were, in fact, building a complicated web of defence across the board.

"This can't be happening. It *can't* be," Oba muttered venomously. But it was. There was nowhere left that he could move his stones without falling deeper into Akori's trap. Blue stone after blue stone was swept from the board until only one was left.

"Just because I was born on a farm, it doesn't mean I'm stupid," said Akori quietly. "And just because you were born in a palace it doesn't mean you're clever." Leaning forward, he moved a red piece, surrounding Oba's final blue stone. As he did so, it began to glow, pulsing with a glimmering magical light that Akori instantly recognized.

His jaw dropped open.

It was a Pharaoh Stone.

Like a flash, his hand moved to take it.

But Oba was quicker. Snatching it from the board, he leaped to his feet. "You still lose, farm boy," he spat. "Did you really think I was going to let your friends live?" Oba turned to the monstrous demon. "Slave, kill them all," he shouted over his shoulder.

A scream of agony rang out behind Akori.

CHAPTER SEVEN

Whirling round, Akori saw Manu struggling in the grip of the demon slave. It stood tall behind him, its face twisted in terrible, ravenous glee. A thin trail of drool ran down its chin as it lifted Manu off his feet, taloned fingers digging into the skin of his shoulder. Its mouth opened to reveal rows of sharp, ripping teeth.

"Leave him alone," Akori screamed, already running towards them. With a feeling of sick horror, he saw the creature lick his lips, as if preparing to feast. Akori touched the Stone of Speed. Power flooded into him, but he was too late. He would not reach Manu in time.

But then the stone floor at the demon slave's feet shattered with a roar that shook the walls. A huge cat flew out from the dungeon beneath, her razor claws raking across the demon's face.

The demon threw Manu to one side and fled from Bast's attack.

Akori kneeled beside Manu and took his head in his lap. Manu's skin was pale and his eyes were closed. "Manu, Manu! Can you hear me?"

Relief flooded through Akori as Manu's eyes flickered open. He struggled to sit up, face ashen. "I-I'm all right," he stuttered. "It looks worse than it is." Looking into Akori's eyes, he managed a smile. "You played a great game of *seega*," he said.

"I'm so sorry I didn't get to you quick enough," Akori said.

Manu snorted. "Don't be silly, you were too far away. Besides, it's just a few scratches. Come on, we need to get out of here."

They both turned their heads as Bast gave a warning growl.

More demon slaves were pouring in from every archway, their slit eyes lit up with hunger.

A slave hurled a spear at Akori. He narrowly missed it, watching as it pierced the ground with lethal force.

"What are we going to do?" Manu cried. "There are so many of them."

Akori looked at the slaves marching towards them, Manu's words ringing in his ears. How could they possibly defeat all of the demons? They would never survive such a vast army.

If you do not think clearly in the Underworld… Well, then you will lose your life. The old priest's words came back to Akori in a rush. *Clear your mind,* he told himself. Akori took a deep breath and recited the old priest's words over and over in his head. He felt a sense of calm flow through him. He looked at the advancing army of demon slaves. Their long, sinewy limbs and razor-sharp claws reminded Akori of the vicious courtyard of cacti. Akori recalled the way the cacti had sliced into each other, rendering them powerless. An idea flashed into his mind, as clear and bright as Ra's sun-barge.

"I've got it!" he cried, grinning at Manu excitedly.

"Halt!" he shouted, brandishing his

khopesh. The slaves carried on marching towards them.

"I said, halt!" Akori yelled. "I am the King of all Egypt. I challenge the strongest amongst you to fight me alone."

The slaves halted and stared at him through their narrow yellow eyes.

"Come on. Which one among you is the most fearless fighter? Which one is the most powerful and most worthy of fighting a Pharaoh?"

Akori held his breath. Next to him, Manu and Ebe stood statue-still as they waited. Two of the demon slaves stepped towards Akori at the same time. Then they turned and stared at each other.

"What are you doing?" one of them hissed. "I am the strongest here."

"You lie!" the other demon snarled. "I am the strongest by far."

"No! I am the strongest," another slave shouted.

"No, I am," called another, shoving him out of the way.

Akori watched with bated breath as the slaves started pushing and shoving. Soon the courtyard rang out with the sound of clashing metal and roars of rage, as, one by one, the slaves began attacking each other with their knives and spears.

"Akori, that is brilliant!" Manu exclaimed. They watched, amazed, as one by one the demons fell, their muscular bodies disintegrating into dust as they slayed each other. Finally, only one figure remained standing – that of the slave who had attacked Manu. But now its armour was dented and its helmet had disappeared. Holding his *khopesh* aloft, Akori charged at the slave. Then at the last second, Akori spun in a rapid roundhouse kick that sent the demon crashing against the wall. It slumped to the ground.

"That's what you get for hurting my friend!" Akori yelled.

The demon let out a final gasp, before crumbling to dust in front of Akori's eyes. He looked around at the rest of the courtyard. The floor was littered with the ashen debris of the slaves.

"At least Oba will never be able to send these demons to invade Egypt," he said.

"That *was* incredible," agreed Manu. "But I'm sure Oba has many other servants. That won't be the last of them."

"Even more reason to collect the last two Pharaoh Stones and finish him for good," said Akori. "Oba had another one with him. A blue stone he used to play *seega*. I think we should find him – and the Stone – before we look for Apep."

"But what about Ra?" asked Manu, frowning.

Akori bit his lip, thinking carefully. Finally he spoke. "Horus said the quest would never be finished unless I have all five of the Pharaoh Stones. But, as Pharaoh, I have to ensure the safety and well-being of my people. You're right, Manu. We should look for Ra first, then find the Stone."

Ebe, now the size of a small cat again, was sitting at Manu's feet, calmly washing the demon dust from her fur. Looking up, she mewed softly.

"Ebe agrees," said Akori, smiling at his friends. But his smile soon faded as he thought of what lay ahead of them. "Are you certain that Apep can only be defeated by a God of equal power?" he asked.

Manu nodded gravely.

Akori gritted his teeth. "Well, as long as we save Ra and get the fourth Pharaoh Stone we will have achieved all that we need to. We don't *need* to defeat Apep. You said he could be found close by. Do you know the way?"

Manu shook his head. "No, but there are instructions on Thoth's scroll that Horus gave us." He unrolled the scroll and stared down at it. "It isn't too far from the palace. Look, we just need to find this pathway and it should lead us right to it."

Akori looked over Manu's shoulder at the scroll. Sure enough, it said that a curving, narrow path stretched to the east of the palace to Apep's lair.

"Let's go," Manu said, wincing slightly as he rolled the scroll back up.

"We're not going anywhere until I've done something about your wounds," Akori said firmly. "Here, let me look at them."

Once Akori had examined Manu's injuries, he tore a strip from the bottom of Manu's tunic and wrapped it round his shoulder like a bandage. "That should do till we get back to the palace," he said.

Manu stood up, looking a lot better than he had a few minutes before. "Thanks," he said with a smile. "Now we really have to go."

Akori looked around as they left Oba's palace. Ahead stretched a featureless desert plain – the sand was as white as salt.

"Bones," Manu whispered, taking a crunching step. "The ground is covered with bones. That's why it's so white."

Akori looked down. A broken skull stared up at him with empty eye sockets. Everywhere he looked there were skulls, ribcages, long leg bones and tiny finger bones tangled together. It looked as if the skeleton of every person who had ever died had been scattered across the plain. Many of the bones were so old they had crumbled into a fine white powder, like sand.

Akori's mouth twisted in disgust.

"We have to walk across it," said Manu.

With a hiss of distaste, Ebe scrambled up Manu's robes. Perching on his unharmed shoulder, she began washing the white powder from her paws.

"At least you don't have to tread on them," Manu sighed to the cat.

Ebe mewed sympathetically.

Trying not to look down, Akori took a step forward. Bones snapped beneath his sandalled feet. "How are we ever going to find the pathway?" he asked.

Manu shrugged. "I don't know. On the scroll it says it is east of the palace."

They all searched the landscape. A clear path wound its way further into the Underworld, but there was no sign of the Snake God. Suddenly Akori cried out. "I think that's it!" In the distance, cutting through the white of the bones, was a narrow green ridged path. "Come on, we have to hurry."

As they began running across the desert of bones, a moaning wind swept in, picking up the white dust and throwing it in their faces. "Could this get any worse?" Manu muttered.

Akori glanced back and saw that Manu's skin and robes had turned completely white, covered in crushed bone. Ebe's fur was the same. And as Akori looked down at his arm, he realized that he was covered in it too. They looked like three ghosts.

Finally, they reached the green pathway. It sloped upwards, like a small hill.

"Maybe once we're up on the pathway we'll be able to see Apep. You wait here and I'll go and check," Akori said, racing ahead.

The green rock of the pathway was cool to the touch. It was covered in overlapping ridges of stone that formed a regular pattern. Watching his step on the smooth surface, Akori walked as quickly as he dared and looked out ahead. The pathway stretched far into the distance. On either side all he could see was the endless white plain.

"I can't see any sign of Apep. Are you sure we came the right way?" he called to Manu below. "Are we definitely headed east of—" Akori let out a cry of shock as the pathway suddenly started shifting beneath his feet. He staggered to one side and then the other as the pathway swayed. Akori looked over at Manu and Ebe.

"Watch out!" he shouted. "I think there's going to be a landslide."

But Manu and Ebe were still standing upright on the bone-covered plain.

Manu started waving his arms about in panic. "Get down. Get down *right now!*" he yelled.

"What is it?" Akori shouted.

Once again, the pathway shifted beneath his feet. Akori stumbled to his hands and knees.

"It's not a landslide," Manu bellowed. "It's Apep. You're standing on his tail!"

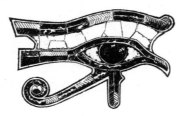

CHAPTER EIGHT

Akori ran along the slippery ridges. They weren't ridges of rock at all, they were *scales – huge scales.* Breathless, he jumped off, his feet crunching on bone as he landed next to Manu. Ebe was skulking behind Manu's legs. Manu's eyes were wide, his jaw hanging open.

"Forty royal cubits," panted Akori. "You said Apep was forty royal cubits long."

"That's only one scroll," Manu replied, without taking his eyes off the enormous tail. "I told you the others said he was bigger than that, remember?"

"How much bigger, exactly?"

Manu shook his head. "I don't know," he answered. "I suppose there's only one way to find out."

Akori gulped. Horus's words came back to him: *"I must warn you, Apep is a terrible foe. When you stand before him, you will need more than courage or speed or strength to save you."* For a split second, he thought about turning back, and running. Surely if they were fast enough they could find a place to hide.

But then he remembered that the people of Egypt were depending on him to bring back the sun. Akori took a deep breath, cleared his mind, and began marching forwards, following the tail. "This is *my* task," he said over his shoulder to Manu and

Ebe. "I won't think any less of you if you choose to go back."

Ebe gave a reproachful meow, as she trotted to catch up with him.

"As if," Manu said, scrambling over broken bones to join them. "Besides, you'll need a High Priest for this battle."

"What for?"

"Well...praying might be a good start."

Despite himself, Akori smiled. Once again he felt a surge of gratitude for having such good friends.

But his smile soon died as they continued to creep alongside Apep's gigantic tail. It stretched on for what looked like hundreds of cubits. Just one flick of it would be enough to crush them to dust like the bones they were walking on. Akori tried to keep a firm grip on his courage. The vast snake's body was getting higher now, and thicker, coiling in on itself in massive loops. How could he hope to defeat something this size? And they hadn't even seen its face yet! Instinctively, his hand went to the hilt of his *khopesh*. *It will be like attacking a crocodile with a pin,* he thought to himself.

"Well, look who's here," said a mocking voice, snapping Akori out of his thoughts. He spun round, to see Oba slide down Apep's scales, a gloating look on his face. *"Just because I was born on a farm, doesn't mean I'm stupid,"* he jeered in a whining mockery of Akori. "But here you are, walking right into my trap. A trap, which I'm delighted to say, you have no hope of escaping. Soon you'll be dead, and, like all the rest of the dead, you'll be mine to do with as I please. Do you want to know what tortures I've invented for you?"

"Will it involve playing *seega* with you?"

asked Akori. "Only I think I'd be bored to death beating you over and over again." He was amazed to find that his voice sounded steady.

Oba's face hardened. "I'll make you *suffer*, you filthy peasant you—"

"Oh, shut up, Oba. You talk too much and your voice is annoying," interrupted Akori. He pulled out his *khopesh* and took a step forward. "Stop playing games and tell me where Ra is."

The sneer returned to Oba's face as he backed away from the point of Akori's sword. "Stupid farm boy. I knew you'd try and rescue him. It's exactly the kind of pathetically heroic thing you'd do. There is no way you'll be able to release him from his prison. Maybe you should look for your precious Stone first? If you want that, all you have to do is take it."

"That won't be a problem," said Akori, taking another step towards him.

"Not from *me*, idiot." Oba was standing in the shadow of the mighty snake now. He reached out and touched the dark green skin. "From my servant." He let out a high-pitched laugh before backing away.

The towering wall of scales moved. A mountain rose from the coils, stretching high into the sky. Suddenly, Akori was staring into slit, yellow eyes, burning with pure evil. Each was bigger than the main gates of his palace. A huge forked tongue the size of a barge flicked out of the monster's mouth, touching Akori, tasting him.

Then Apep opened his jaws.

It was as if the earth itself had opened up. Akori took a step back, his knees threatening to buckle as he gazed, horrified, down Apep's throat. High above, fangs the size of obelisks

dripped great pools of venom onto the sand.

Terrified, but fascinated, Akori's eyes fixed on a slim silver collar around Apep's throat. In the very centre was a tiny blue glimmer.

The Pharaoh Stone!

As if reading Akori's thoughts, Apep hissed, daring him to come and take it. A gale of rancid breath sent Akori tumbling and rolling through the sand.

"As traps go, I have to say, it's a good one," said Oba, lightly. "I'll leave Apep to play with you now – I have some new tortures to prepare. Soon, you'll be here in the Underworld for good, and I'll have all eternity to teach you about misery. Goodbye, for now, farm boy."

Oba walked away.

Akori turned to Manu. "H-how can I defeat *this*?" he asked.

Manu's eyes were wide with fear. He was speechless.

Akori turned to face Apep again. With another hiss the huge head reared back. Apep was preparing to strike. Deep within the giant snake's endless coils, Akori glimpsed a struggling being that had the shape of a man but which glowed with the pure rays of the sun: it was Ra, trapped by his ageless enemy.

Akori took a deep breath. He had to save Ra if it was the last thing he did. Without the mighty Sun God all Egypt would wither and die. He had worked out ways to defeat the army of cacti and the demon slaves. He just had to think, and surely there would be an answer here too? But before Akori could think of a single thing, Apep's massive head streaked down from above, jaws open to seize his tiny prey.

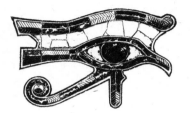

CHAPTER NINE

"Move!" Akori yelled. Pushing Manu in one direction, he snatched Ebe and hurled himself in the other. He felt hot breath burn his back.

The ground shook. Apep's jaws closed around nothing but dry bone dust. The great snake reared again, hissing and shaking his head. Torrents of dust fell from his jaws, falling on Akori, covering him. He struggled free, spitting dust from his mouth.

At his side, the ground swelled. Ebe rose as

Bast, shaking white bone dust from her fur, her mouth opening in a roar of challenge.

"Ebe, *no*! We can't beat him in a straight fight," yelled Akori as she crouched, ready to pounce, the roar swelling in her throat. She was huge now, but still a tiny kitten compared to Apep.

The giant head snaked down. At the last moment, Bast sprang at Apep's snout. Her claws raked the scales, clinging to it like a cat climbing a tree.

In a second, Apep had shaken her off. Akori's blood froze as he watched her smash into the ground, making a deep gouge in the bones as she tumbled. "Ebe!" he shouted, running towards her.

In answer, Bast staggered to her feet. She glanced at him, and nodded. Somehow, the cat always managed to communicate her thoughts to him and there was no mistaking what Bast meant now: *It's all right. I'm buying you some time.* Then she .was gone, bounding through the sand towards Apep once more.

Akori turned to his friend. "Manu," he gasped, pulling him to his feet. "Is there something in the scroll? A way to defeat Apep? A spell? Anything?"

Manu shook his head, eyes fixed on the snake's head above. Apep struck again, snapping at Bast. "There's nothing," he said. "Only a God of equal or greater power can battle Apep and hope to win."

A massive shriek of rage ripped through the air. Apep reared higher and higher, writhing and hissing and ready to strike.

Clutching Manu's arm, Akori ran. Again, Apep found nothing but a mouthful of dust.

"There's nothing else for it then," Akori

shouted back. "I'm going to have to fight him myself."

"Akori, don't! That's not the way..."

Akori was already gone, his feet throwing up clouds of bone dust as he raced towards Apep, shouting, "You missed again you stupid, oversized worm."

Apep stopped. He blinked, regarding Akori with sudden interest, tongue flickering in and out.

Akori gripped his *khopesh*, hoping that Apep couldn't see his arm shaking. "Want another go?" he called up. But inside he was quaking. Reaching for his collar, he touched the Stone of Courage and felt instantly reassured by its power.

Jaws open wide, the snake's head screamed down. Akori grabbed hold of the Stone of Speed. His legs blurred as he raced out of Apep's path. A wall of green scales smashed into the ground beside him. Jumping to his feet, Akori shot up the huge snake's head. When he got to the top he touched the final Stone. Strength tore through his body like fire. He raised the *khopesh* with both hands and plunged it into Apep's snout as easily as if he was slicing through water.

Gripping the hilt of the *khopesh*, which was still embedded in Apep's slimy scales, Akori rose into the sky as Apep reared back, shrieking. Pulling the *khopesh* free, Akori clambered higher up the head, until he stood, looking into one of Apep's massive eyes as wind and cloud streamed around him. "You may be big," he bellowed. "But I'm still going to take you down."

Apep's bellow of rage echoed across the Underworld. He shook his head, as if trying to rid himself of an annoying insect with a

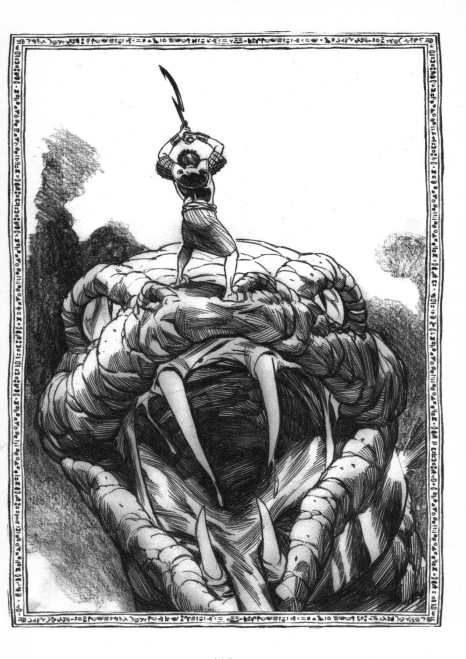

tiny sting. Akori sank the *khopesh* into the snake's flesh again and hung on for dear life.

A second later, he was descending fast, as Apep lowered his great head. He rubbed it against the ground, trying to scrape Akori off. Teeth gritted, eyes squeezed shut against the billowing dust, Akori clung on.

"Think!" he heard Manu shout in the distance. "Use your intelligence."

"I'm trying!" Akori yelled back. Desperately, he tried to clear his mind. He thought about what Manu had said about a God of equal or greater power...

A God of equal power.

Yes!

Akori suddenly knew what he had to do. Quick as a lightning bolt, he steadied himself between Apep's eyes once more. Stopping for a moment, he looked down. The snake's scaled body sloped away into coils below –

stretching away to the tip that Akori had mistaken for the footpath before.

With a quick prayer to all the good Gods, Akori leaped from the snake's head and threw himself down its neck.

The scales were oily, slippery beneath his feet. He half ran, half skated down them, at a speed that brought tears to his eyes. Knowing that if he slipped he was dead, he concentrated on keeping his balance. It wasn't easy. Feeling Akori fleeing down his own body, Apep writhed, trying to dislodge him. Once, twice, he struck, forcing Akori to dodge. Again and again, Apep's jaws closed on empty air. Then, suddenly, his teeth clamped down on his own tail, narrowly missing Akori. Opening his massive jaws to the sky, the God shrieked in pain and rage.

Keep him angry, Akori told himself. "Stupid snake," he yelled. "Can't kill one puny little human? What kind of a ridiculous God are you?"

He ducked as the jaws passed by again, Apep's foul breath almost flattening him. The slope was less steep now as Akori clambered up the great beast. He had almost reached the coils that Apep had thrown around Ra, keeping him imprisoned. They tightened and Akori could no longer see the glow of Ra's light. Akori guessed that Apep was afraid he was trying to release the Sun God. Akori would need to distract Apep. Putting on an extra burst of speed, he leaped from one coil to the next, moving further and further back down Apep's long body. "Nearly there," he panted. Just ahead was the tip of Apep's thrashing tail.

Made it!

Skidding to a stop, Akori plunged his *khopesh* into the snake's scales. It sank up to the hilt. Apep shrieked again, the tail whipping back and forth. Akori gripped tight. Going down on one knee, he raised his head and shouted, "Hey, Apep. No wonder Oba keeps losing with servants like you."

The screaming head lunged at him. Akori flattened himself against the scales.

Come on: one more time.

"Is this why Ra beats you at the end of every day? Because you're completely useless?"

Apep's coils began to unwind. In his fury, the monstrous snake snapped and hissed at his own whipping tail.

"You only beat Ra this time because Set helped you."

With a screech, Apep lunged. Dragging his *khopesh* out, Akori ran back the way he had come. For a second, he felt hot breath on his back and then the mighty jaws snapped closed as Apep tore at his tail once more.

Akori whirled round, punching the air. His plan was working! But there was no time to celebrate. Darting forward, he jabbed at Apep with the *khopesh*, yelling, "I fought Sokar and Baal and Babi. They were all quite tough. Oba must be running out of decent allies if he's been forced to use you this time."

With a roar, Apep lunged forward again, his tongue darting towards Akori. But Akori was too fast, and again, the great beast attacked his own flesh. Akori danced backwards, enjoying himself now. "I wonder what I'll have to fight next," he laughed, "A dung beetle?"

Enraged, Apep snapped at him, again and again. But every time, Akori dodged out of the way. The huge snake was maddened with frustration, rearing up in pain and anger. Spitting venom, in a burst of fury, Apep lunged at Akori. His skin sizzled as the snake's poison spattered him.

Apep's fangs narrowly missed the young Pharaoh. But the Snake God had attacked with such speech and force, that his almighty mouth closed around his own tail. Apep choked, trying to cough it out, but it was wedged in too far. He writhed and slithered but to no avail. The Snake God had swallowed his own tail.

Coolly, Akori stepped forward and patted the snout that rose above him. Apep glared at him, his eyes burning with hatred.

"Only a God of equal power could beat you," Akori said, quietly. "And that God was you."

CHAPTER TEN

Akori slid along Apep's neck. Halfway down he saw a blue glimmer from the collar around the snake's throat. He reached out and closed his fingers around the fourth Pharaoh Stone.

Instantly, he felt his brain start to tingle. His mind cleared. Things he hadn't understood before now seemed amazingly simple. Opening his fingers, he gazed at the twinkling Stone in his palm. "Intelligence," he whispered. He placed the Stone in his collar and slid down to the ground.

"You did it. You did it!"

Akori turned to see Manu running towards him with a huge grin on his face. Ebe bounded along at his side, shrinking to her normal size as she leaped onto Akori's shoulder. A rough tongue licked his face. Ebe's throat rumbled with a purr of love and pride.

"That was amazing. It will go down in history," Manu shouted, throwing his arms around Akori's shoulders. "No one but Ra has ever defeated Apep."

"Ra!" shouted Akori. "He's still trapped."

Apep's coils shifted. For a second Akori thought the Snake God was about to wriggle free but, with a heave, a golden man stepped out from between the coils. His skin was as gold as wheat and a halo glowed around his head.

"Not any longer, thanks to you, Akori," he said. For a moment, Ra glanced back at Apep.

"You performed a mighty task," he said. "But Apep will rise again. At night I will battle him once more. Without Set's aid, he will lose. As he always loses." Striding forward, the God bowed to Akori. "We meet again, Pharaoh of Egypt. And again, I owe you my gratitude." Then he bowed to Manu. "My thanks to you, also, High Priest of Horus, and to you Bast, my old friend." Reaching out to Akori's shoulder he scratched Ebe's ears. She pushed her head against his glowing hand, purring.

"No thanks are necessary," replied Akori, grinning. He liked the Sun God enormously. Ra's warm smile lit up the world. Even the gloomy Underworld suddenly seemed a brighter place. "My people need you."

"Your people are lucky to have such a King. As you care for them so much, it is your people I will reward. For as long as you sit upon the throne of Egypt they will have harvests like they have never seen before."

Akori's grin grew wider. "A magnificent gift, My Lord Ra," he said. "But right now they are frightened. Egypt is in darkness."

Ra nodded. "I will return to my rightful place immediately. May I offer you aid in your own journey home?"

Akori's shoulders sagged with relief. "Please," he murmured.

"Then let us leave this place." Reaching out, Ra placed one hand on Akori's shoulder, another on Manu's. A swirl of golden light surrounded them. Akori felt a breath of warmth on his face, like the kiss of a summer breeze. He blinked and saw a huge boat emerging from the darkness. It was painted gold and a brilliant white sail billowed behind it.

Akori and Manu exchanged grins.

They had seen this boat before.

"Your sun-barge!" Akori exclaimed.

Ra nodded and smiled.

The boat drew up beside them and they clambered on board. Ra took his place at the tiller, his halo growing brighter with every second.

On the ground next to them Apep writhed and hissed, but his tail remained wedged in his mouth.

"Until next time!" Ra called to his deadly foe. Then he pulled the tiller round. Akori and Manu held onto the edge of the boat while Ebe curled at their feet. Faster and faster Ra's barge raced through the Underworld in a blaze of bright white light.

"Hold tight!" Ra shouted as they shot out from the jaws of the Underworld and began climbing into the sky.

"We made it!" Manu shouted.

Akori smiled as he leaned over the side of the boat.

Way down below him he saw people the size of ants begin running out into the fields, crying with delight at the return of the sun.

Ra followed the course of the Nile until Akori's palace came into sight. As Ra lowered the barge Akori saw that the palace courtyard was swarming with servants and guards. The air was filled with the sound of their stamping feet and clapping hands. Beyond the palace walls, the people of Thebes had joined them. It sounded as if the whole of Egypt had lifted its voice in gratitude and joy.

"Farewell, courageous Pharaoh," Ra said to Akori before pointing downwards. A shaft of golden light shone, forming a bridge from his hand to the ground. Akori, Manu and Ebe carefully walked down it into the palace courtyard.

"Farewell, mighty Ra!" Akori called as the sun-barge took off into the sky. The cheers of the servants and guards reached a deafening roar.

Blushing, Akori followed their gaze upward. The brilliant blue of the sky was a beautiful sight after the darkness of the Underworld. The sun beat down with gentle warmth. *Good weather for the crops*, Akori thought with a smile.

Lowering his gaze, he saw the crowd part. The old High Priest hobbled through, leaning on a stick.

"You make an old man very proud," he said, coming to a halt in front of Akori. "And you fill me with hope for the future of Egypt."

Akori's blush deepened. "Thank you," he said, not knowing quite how to reply.

The old High Priest reached out and

touched the blue Pharaoh Stone at Akori's throat. "Intelligence," he wheezed. "A fitting Stone for the conqueror of Apep. I look forward to hearing how it was won."

"It was incredible," Manu blurted. "We had to fight Bukhu – *again* – then we saw off an army of killer cacti and Akori whipped Oba at *seega*, then he fought the demon slaves, and you should have *seen* the way he defeated Apep! He tricked him into eating his own tail!"

The old man's face suddenly looked young again, lighting up in a huge smile. "Manu, let me hear the story properly, over some food perhaps? You must all be hungry after your adventure."

Ebe meowed, and jumped to the old man's shoulder.

"Yes, there will be a fresh fish just for you, Ebe," he chuckled.

"Anything," interrupted the chief servant, stepping forward. "The staff – all the people – wish to give thanks to their Pharaoh. I will see to it that the kitchens produce a feast like Egypt has never before seen."

Akori thanked him, realizing how hungry he was. The chief servant strode off and slowly the courtyard began to clear. "Before we eat, you're going to see the palace doctor," Akori told Manu. "I want those wounds looked at properly."

"I'll be fine…" Manu began.

Akori held up a hand. "That's an order from your Pharaoh," he said, kindly, but firmly.

As Manu left, Akori sank onto a stone bench, exhausted. A hand touched his shoulder.

"What is it, my Pharaoh?" asked the old priest.

Akori looked up into his milky white eyes. "This quest," he said slowly. "It was the most difficult yet. There was a moment when I just wanted to turn and run."

The old priest smiled gently. "But you didn't. You beat Apep. Only Ra has ever managed that."

"Yes, but now I have four of the Pharaoh Stones, Oba will do everything in his power to stop me getting the last. I'm worried that I'll fail."

The old priest's fingers gripped his shoulder gently. "You will face Oba again, but I believe in you. All the people of Egypt believe in you."

Akori shook his head. "What if I let them down?" he whispered.

The old priest nodded gravely. "There is no doubt that the worst is yet to come. Oba and Set will be intent upon putting their evil plan into action as soon as they can. And their army will be growing ever more powerful. But do not forget – you have been able to thwart them four times now."

Akori looked up and nodded. "Yes," he said, as courage and hope began returning to him. "You're right. Oba *has* failed four times. And surely there is nothing he can unleash that is worse than Apep." He placed his hand on the old priest's shoulder and gave a determined smile. "Nothing will stop me from saving Osiris and all Egypt now!"

EPILOGUE

"No!" screeched Oba, clutching his hair. "It's not possible. No one can beat Apep." He kicked out, overturning the copper dish of fire. "He was supposed to die," he wailed as flames spread across the floor of his throne room. "I want him to die. Why will he not just die?"

A demon slave stepped forward, nervously. "My Lord, you must not upset yourself…"

"Shut up. I did not give you permission to speak." Oba's clenched fist smashed into the side of the slave's head, sending it reeling away, shrieking in pain.

"Oba," boomed a deep voice. "Once again you have disappointed me."

Spinning around, Oba saw Set walk out of the flames, a hideous snarl on his face.

Oba's knees almost buckled. "It wasn't my fault," he whispered. "It was Apep. Stupid, stupid Apep. The pathetic snake swallowed his own tail. It was Akori he was supposed to eat. It wasn't my fault. No one could blame me."

"I *blame* you."

Oba's hands dropped, shocked by the venom in Set's voice. "My-my L-Lord Set—" he stammered.

"YOU WILL BE SILENT!" Lumps of rock fell from the ceiling at the sound of Set's voice, smashing into thousands of pieces as they hit the ground.

Oba stared.

"Once again you have let this false Pharaoh slip through your fingers," Set continued with quiet menace. "We are running out of allies and we are running out of time."

Forcing himself to smile, Oba said, "Next time, Lord Set. You'll see. I'll ki—"

"I SAID, SILENCE!"

Oba's jaw snapped shut.

"For you there will be no next time," sneered Set. "I have allowed you to fail too many times already. Now, I will take charge." His voice changed, becoming quiet. "Akori must return for the fifth Pharaoh Stone. When he does, he will find no ordinary God waiting for him."

"Wh-what…what are you going to do, Lord Set?" asked Oba, fingers twisting together with nerves.

Set faced the flames. For a moment he didn't answer, and then he turned his head, glaring at Oba. "I am going to do what should have been done in the first place," he said. "I am going to feed his soul to the Devourer!"

DON'T MISS AKORI'S FINAL BATTLE!

QUEST of the GODS

DESCENT OF THE SOUL DESTROYER

Akori faces the ultimate challenge as he prepares to battle Ammit, the monstrous Soul Devourer. Can he succeed before Oba's army of the dead destroys Egypt for ever?

READ ON FOR A SNEAK PREVIEW!

The wind howled again, even louder and more menacing than before.

Akori shuddered. "It sounds like a thousand voices, crying out into the night..." He stopped mid-sentence. Then he grabbed a burning torch, strode over to one of the many shuttered windows and flung it open.

Manu ran to his side, alarmed. "What are you doing?"

"Look!" Akori held the torch outside so that Manu could see. The flame didn't flicker at all, and Akori couldn't feel a breath of wind on his face. None of the buildings he could see from the window were covered in sand, like they would normally be in a desert storm. In fact, they seemed in perfect condition.

"The air's completely still," Manu said,

with a look of dawning horror. "There's no wind at all."

The endless moaning now rose to a crescendo, seeming to rush in on them from everywhere. Akori could even make out individual voices in the morass of noise – screams, groans, roars of rage, sobs of grief.

Ebe leaped from the old High Priest's lap onto the table, arched her back and hissed.

The High Priest stood and raised a shaking hand. "Gods be with us all."

"The dead!" Akori gasped. "It must be the dead howling from the Underworld."

WILL AKORI DEFEAT OBA BEFORE THE ARMY OF THE DEAD INVADES EGYPT?

JOIN AKORI FOR HIS DEADLIEST BATTLE YET IN...

DESCENT OF THE SOUL DESTROYER

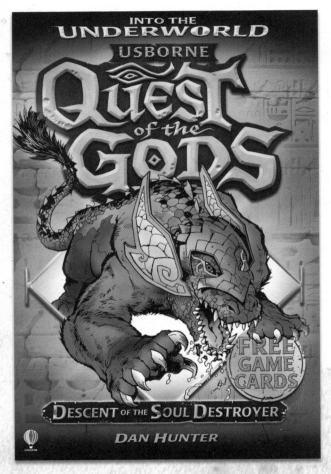

ISBN 9781409562085

OUT NOW!

COLLECT EVERY UNDERWORLD ADVENTURE:

FIGHT *OF THE* FALCON GOD

Akori must venture into the
dark and deadly Underworld to
battle the fearsome Falcon God.
But will he make it out alive?

ISBN 9781409562009

RISE *OF THE*
HORNED WARRIOR

Akori must journey to the
Underworld labyrinth of bones
and fight the lightning-fast Lord of
Thunder. Can he match the God's
awesome speed?

ISBN 9781409562023

SCREAM *OF THE*
BABOON KING

With dark magic invading the
land, Akori must find the terrifying
creature stalking his nightmares –
the bloodthirsty Baboon God!

ISBN 9781409562047

CATCH UP WITH ALL OF AKORI'S QUESTS!

EVIL PHARAOH OBA HAS IMPRISONED THE GODS WHO PROTECT EGYPT, AND NOW BLOODTHIRSTY MONSTERS ROAM THE LAND.

ONLY ONE BOY CAN STOP THEM...

ATTACK OF THE SCORPION RIDERS

For his first quest, Akori must risk his life, fighting giant scorpions and a deadly Snake Goddess. But will his terrifying battle end in victory?

ISBN 97814095621051

CURSE OF THE DEMON DOG

The dead are stalking the living and Akori must send them back to their graves. But dog-headed Am-Heh the Hunter has sworn to destroy Akori...and no one has ever escaped his fearsome jaws.

ISBN 97814095621068

BATTLE OF THE CROCODILE KING

Akori must brave the crocodile-infested waters of the Nile to battle two evil gods – the terrifying Crocodile King, and his gruesome wife, the Frog Goddess – both hungry for his blood...

ISBN 97814095621075

LAIR OF THE WINGED MONSTER

Vicious vultures and deadly beasts lie in wait for Akori as he searches the desert for the Hidden Fortress of Fire – and the Goddess imprisoned there. Will he survive or will this quest be his last...?

ISBN 9781409521082

SHADOW OF THE STORM LORD

The battle to end all battles has begun. Akori must fight Set, the dark Lord of Storms himself, and beat Oba, the evil Pharaoh, to claim his rightful throne. But can Egypt's young hero finally win the crown?

ISBN 97814095621099

FREE GAME CARDS IN EVERY BOOK!

EACH BOOK IN QUEST OF THE GODS
INTO THE UNDERWORLD
COMES WITH AN EXCLUSIVE PHARAOH STONE CARD

- Each Pharaoh Stone card is worth a number of bonus points. The further in the series you get, the more powerful the Pharaoh Stone card in the book, and the more bonus points available:

> Book 6: Stone of Courage = 50 points
> Book 7: Stone of Speed = 150 points
> Book 8: Stone of Strength = 250 points
> Book 9: Stone of Intelligence = 350 points
> Book 10: Stone of Honour = 450 points

Five-Card Trick

Players: 2

Number of cards: 10+ standard cards, and all 5 Pharaoh Stone cards from books 6-10

Dice: 1

Instructions:

- Shuffle the pack and deal the standard cards face down to the players. Place all five Pharaoh Stone cards in the centre of the table. Roll a dice to see who starts.
- *Player One*: select a category from your topmost card and roll for a bonus, adding it to your score if you roll the corresponding number shown on the card for that category.
- *Player Two*: read out the stat of the same category from your cards and also roll for a bonus.
- The player with the highest score wins the round and collects the first Pharaoh Stone Card of Courage.
- *WIN*: Players must win five consecutive battles, picking up each Pharaoh Stone Card in order of their appearance in the books to win the game.
- *LOSE*: If a player with more than one consecutive win loses a battle, all their Pharaoh Stone cards are returned to the centre of the table and they must start again from zero.

FOR MORE FANTASTIC GAMES, GO TO WWW.QUESTOFTHEGODS.CO.UK